Sky Sweeper

Phillis Gershator

Pictures by Holly Meade

Melanie Kroupa Books
Farrar, Straus and Giroux New York

Young Takeboki needed a job,
and the monks in the temple needed
a Flower Keeper.

It was the Flower Keeper's job
to sweep up the springtime plum
and cherry blossoms in the
temple garden.

Takeboki swept up all the fallen flowers,
but when spring passed into summer,
no one told him to stop sweeping.

He swept through summer, fall,

and winter, too.

And then it was spring again.

One year went by, and another, and his parents said, "Son, you're getting too old to be a Flower Keeper. Why don't you look for a better job? There is no future in sweeping."

"I'm happy sweeping," he told his parents, though he thought it might be nice to have a more important-sounding job.

But he knew what he knew: *The monks need a temple, the temple needs a garden, and the garden needs a Flower Keeper.*

My job *does* have a future, he thought. I sweep in every season, and every season follows the one before!

Takeboki's older brother asked,
"Why don't you find a job like mine?
Someday I will own my own shop. I will
make a lot of money and visit faraway places."

"I'm happy sweeping," Takeboki said,
though he often thought of faraway places.

But he knew what he knew: *The monks need a temple, the temple needs a garden, and the garden needs a Flower Keeper.*

"I do go places," he told his brother. "Mysterious islands, deep dark pine forests, snow-covered volcanoes—all here in one small garden!"

In the summertime, Takeboki raked straight lines in the sand and curved lines in the gravel. "Doesn't the sand remind you of the sea?" he asked one of the monks. "Doesn't the gravel around the rocks remind you of water swirling around an ocean reef? If I place one flower on this sandy sea, the petals will drift in the breeze, like boats sailing away."

The monk said nothing. He was thinking his own thoughts and paid no attention to the Flower Keeper.

Takeboki never spoke again of the many worlds he saw when he looked at the garden, but he kept creating them.

When Takeboki got a little older, his sister said, "Why don't you look for a wife? There will be nobody left to marry by the time you get around to it."

"I'm happy sweeping," he said, though he admired the ladies in their brightly colored kimonos. It would be nice to hold someone's soft hand in my own, he thought. Maybe I will get around to hand-holding one day.

But he knew what he knew: *The monks need a temple, the temple needs a garden, and the garden needs a Flower Keeper.*

"It's spring again," he reminded his sister, "time to sweep up the cherry blossoms and tend to the peonies, the loveliest ladies in the garden."

When he got still older, his neighbors said, "Takeboki, look at you—you look like a beggar!"

"I may look like a beggar," he said, "but I'm rich! It's autumn again, and I have more gold than I can carry!"

Takeboki swept up the golden leaves piled on the pathways.
Once the paths were spotless, he left behind a single leaf,
marking the change of seasons with one last reminder of fall.

When he was very old, and his back was bent, the gossips talked among themselves. "Poor old Takeboki," one said. "He must be sorry he was only a Flower Keeper all his life." Another agreed. "He never had a good job. He never married or had children. All he did was sweep, sweep, sweep. And he says he's happy!"

Takeboki heard what the gossips said, but he knew what he knew: *The monks need a temple, the temple needs a garden, and the garden needs a Flower Keeper.* And as long as his legs carried him to work, he *was* happy.

A year passed, and the Flower Keeper grew too old and sick to go to work. At first, the monks didn't even realize he was gone.

Then, in the summer, sticks littered the sand.

In the fall, leaves piled up on the ground.

In the winter, snow
hid the stone paths.

And in the spring,
fallen blossoms turned
to muddy carpets.

"Where is the Flower
Keeper?" the monks
asked one another.

"I believe," said the most eminent monk,
"that the Flower Keeper accomplished more
than we realized. Our garden was famous for its perfection. Have you noticed how few people visit the temple these days? I myself do not study and pray with the same peace of mind. We must find the Flower Keeper. We need him!"

The monks made their way to the poor section of town, where small wooden houses pressed against one another.

There they found Takeboki's dwelling. Inside, the old Flower Keeper lay on his bed. "Are we too late?" cried the monks.

"Yes," said the most eminent monk. "I'm afraid we are. We're too late to tell the Flower Keeper how much we need him. Now he's gone. But look! He has a smile on his face. Remember the Buddha's simple truth? A single flower says more than words. Our Flower Keeper never heard us say the words 'Thank you for what you have given us,' but he heard the flowers. And now, like the Buddha, he smiles."

Takeboki had left this world, but he entered a new one—a radiant land without end. And to his great delight, a golden rake appeared in his right hand and a silver broom in his left. Lifting the precious tools to his shoulder, he turned to look in each of the four directions.

"Where shall I begin?"

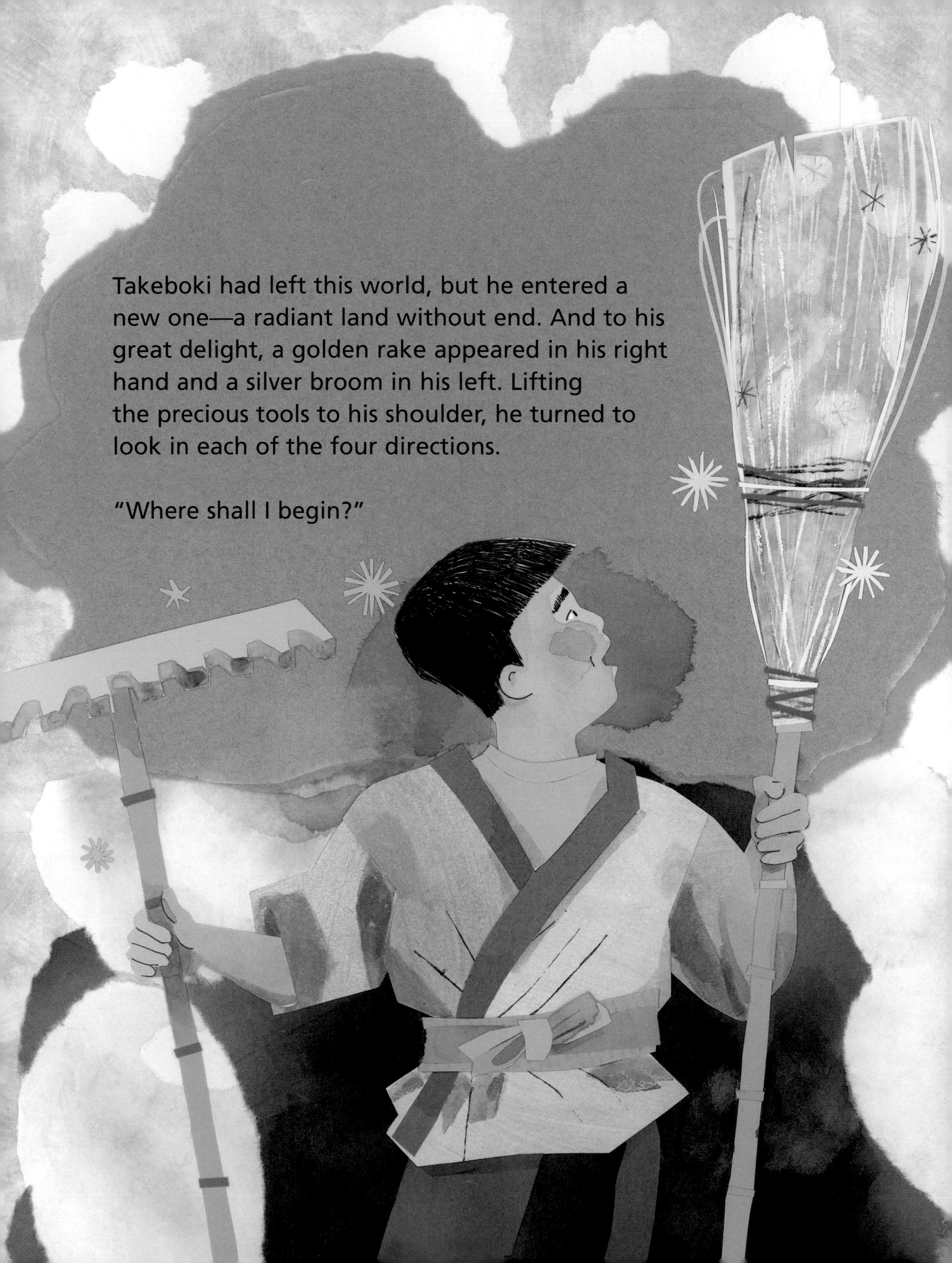

In the south, Takeboki swept clouds into billowing mountains and shifting, drifting wisps of white.

In the west, he raked clouds through the day's last rays—
how fiery the setting sun!

In the north, he swept shimmering curtains across the sky—
how bright the dark of night!

In the east, he swept mist over the moon's face—
how full the hidden moon!

Takeboki smiled again, knowing what he knew.

In the temple garden,
the new Flower Keeper
rakes and sweeps—
and smiles, too.

落花枝に
歸ると見れば
胡蝶かな

A fallen blossom
returns to the branch—
ah, a butterfly!
—Moritake

Author's Note

I once lived across the street from the Brooklyn Botanic Garden. My favorite part of the park was and always will be its authentic Japanese Garden, especially when the cherry blossoms are in bloom. The garden features a pond with a viewing pavilion—a good spot to watch ducks, birds, turtles, and colorful koi. There is also a path around the lake leading to a waterfall, a shrine among the pines, and benches where you can sit and meditate, or read and write haiku. For me, this exquisite garden within a garden is a spirit-lifting refuge—peaceful, serene, yet lively, too.

Brooklyn's Japanese Garden is a classical Hill-and-Pond-style garden, considered the most beautiful of its kind in the Western Hemisphere. The Hill-and-Pond style, influenced by the gardens of Korea and China, goes back at least to the eighth century A.D. Another traditional style, the sand-and-rock garden, called Dry Landscape, contains no water and few plants: the rocks represent islands and mountains, the sand takes the place of water, and a bit of moss might symbolize green hills or valleys. The Dry Landscape garden is most often associated with Zen Buddhism. Ever since the thirteenth century, this popular offshoot of Buddhism has had a strong influence on Japanese calligraphy, poetry, painting—and the art of gardening. Both styles, Hill-and-Pond and Dry Landscape, are pictured in *Sky Sweeper*.

The artistry of Japanese gardens, the traditional job of Flower Keeper, and the idea that honest work has value, recognized or not, inspired this tale of Takeboki, whose name comes from the Japanese word for bamboo broom: *take-bōki*. His life after death reflects the belief of one of the most popular Buddhist sects, Pure Land Buddhism, that rebirth in a blissful paradise is possible. Paradise, for Takeboki, is a place where the joy of work never ends.

To David, Karen, Kaylan, Michiko, Masako, Melanie, Mimi—and especially to Holly Meade for her help in telling this story and shaping its messages. Thank you! —P.G.

For all the children who hear a different drummer. Wishing you the courage to follow that which you hear. —H.M.

William J. Higginson's translation of "A fallen blossom" by Arakida Moritake (Japanese, 1473–1549) was prepared especially for *Sky Sweeper*.

Distributed in Canada by Douglas & McIntyre Ltd.
Color separations by Embassy Graphics
Printed and bound in China by South China Printing Co. Ltd.
Designed by Jay Colvin
First edition, 2007
1 3 5 7 9 10 8 6 4 2

www.fsgkidsbooks.com

Library of Congress Cataloging-in-Publication Data
Gershator, Phillis.
Sky sweeper / Phillis Gershator ; pictures by Holly Meade.— 1st ed.
p. cm.
Summary: Despite criticism for his lack of "accomplishments," Takeboki finds contentment sweeping the flower blossoms and raking the sand and gravel in the monks' temple garden. Includes a note on the art and beauty of Japanese gardens.
ISBN-13: 978-0-374-37007-7
ISBN-10: 0-374-37007-9
[1. Gardens, Japanese—Fiction. 2. Work—Fiction. 3. Contentment—Fiction. 4. Self-actualization (Psychology)—Fiction. 5. Zen Buddhism—Fiction. 6. Japan—Fiction.]
I. Meade, Holly, ill. II. Title.

PZ7.G316 Sk 2007
[E]—dc22

2005049762